Dear Parents and Educators,

Welcome to Penguin Young Readers! As parents and educators, you know that each child develops at his or her own pace—in terms of speech, critical thinking, and, of course, reading. Penguin Young Readers recognizes this fact. As a result, each Penguin Young Readers book is assigned a traditional easy-to-read level (1–4) as well as a Guided Reading Level (A–P). Both of these systems will help you choose the right book for your child. Please refer to the back of each book for specific leveling information. Penguin Young Readers features esteemed authors and illustrators, stories about favorite characters, fascinating nonfiction, and more!

Young Cam Jansen and the Magic Bird Mystery

LEVEL 3

GUIDED READING LEVEL **J**

This book is perfect for a **Transitional Reader** who:
- can read multisyllable and compound words;
- can read words with prefixes and suffixes;
- is able to identify story elements (beginning, middle, end, plot, setting, characters, problem, solution); and
- can understand different points of view.

Here are some **activities** you can do during and after reading this book:
- Comprehension: Using her amazing memory, Cam is finally able to solve the mystery of Teddy's missing bird, Oscar. Once you've finished the book, use *your* amazing memory to explain to a friend or parent what happened to Oscar.
- Find all the words in the story that have an -ed ending. On a separate sheet of paper, write the root word next to the word with the -ed ending. The chart below will get you started:

word with an -ed ending	root word
bowed	bow
cheered	cheer

Remember, sharing the love of reading with a child is the best gift you can give!

—Bonnie Bader, EdM.
  Penguin Young Readers program

*Penguin Young Readers are leveled by independent reviewers applying the standards developed by Irene Fountas and Gay Su Pinnell in *Matching Books to Readers: Using Leveled Books in Guided Reading*, Heinemann, 1999.

For Ruth and Murray.
Hi Ho, Silvers!—DA

To Hannah Rose, Mason, and Oliver—SN

Penguin Young Readers
Published by the Penguin Group
Penguin Group (USA) Inc., 375 Hudson Street, New York, New York 10014, USA
Penguin Group (Canada), 90 Eglinton Avenue East, Suite 700, Toronto, Ontario M4P 2Y3, Canada
(a division of Pearson Penguin Canada Inc.)
Penguin Books Ltd, 80 Strand, London WC2R 0RL, England
Penguin Ireland, 25 St Stephen's Green, Dublin 2, Ireland (a division of Penguin Books Ltd)
Penguin Group (Australia), 707 Collins Street, Melbourne, Victoria 3008, Australia
(a division of Pearson Australia Group Pty Ltd)
Penguin Books India Pvt Ltd, 11 Community Centre, Panchsheel Park, New Delhi—110 017, India
Penguin Group (NZ), 67 Apollo Drive, Rosedale, Auckland 0632, New Zealand (a division of Pearson New Zealand Ltd)
Penguin Books (South Africa), Rosebank Office Park, 181 Jan Smuts Avenue, Parktown North 2193, South Africa
Penguin China, B7 Jiaming Center, 27 East Third Ring Road North, Chaoyang District, Beijing 100020, China

Penguin Books Ltd, Registered Offices: 80 Strand, London WC2R 0RL, England

Text copyright © 2012 by David A. Adler. Illustrations copyright © 2012 by Susanna Natti. All rights reserved. Previously
published in hardcover in 2012 by Penguin Young Readers. This edition published in 2013 by Penguin Young Readers,
an imprint of Penguin Group (USA) Inc., 345 Hudson Street, New York, New York 10014. Manufactured in China.

Library of Congress Control Number: 2011028216

ISBN 978-0-448-46613-2   10 9 8 7 6 5 4 3

PENGUIN YOUNG READERS

LEVEL
3
TRANSITIONAL
READER

Young Cam Jansen
and the Magic Bird Mystery

by David A. Adler
illustrated by Susanna Natti

Penguin Young Readers
An Imprint of Penguin Group (USA) Inc.

Contents

Chapter 1
Let's See Some Magic

"Lots of times my friend Teddy
reached behind my ear
and pulled out pennies,"
said Aunt Molly.

"Wow!" Cam Jansen said.

"That's magic!"

"Wow nothing," Molly said.

"I told him to pull out dollars."

"Here's his store," Eric Shelton said.

"Here's Teddy's Toys."

"Teddy and I worked together
at the airline a long time ago,"
Molly told Cam and Eric.

They all went into Teddy's Toys.
They walked past a large sign
with arrows.

It told shoppers where to find things.

"Teddy once reached behind my ear and pulled out an airplane ticket."

"Wow!" Eric said.

"Wow nothing," Molly said again.

"It was a ticket to Paris. I'd already been there."

"This is a really big store," Eric said.

"Where's the magic show?" Aunt Molly asked.

"Cam knows," Eric said.

Cam closed her eyes and said, "Click!"

She looked at the picture in her head of the sign with the arrows.

"To the left are riding toys,

video games, and snacks," Cam said.

"They have popcorn, ice cream,

and drinks."

Cam Jansen has an

amazing memory.

Her memory is like a camera with

pictures of everything she's seen.

"But where's the magic show?"

Aunt Molly asked.

"It's in the party room," Cam said.
"That's straight ahead."

Cam says, "Click!" when she wants
to remember something.
She says that *click!* is the sound
her mental camera makes.
Cam's real name is Jennifer,
but when people found out
about her great memory,
they called her "the Camera."

Soon "the Camera"

became just "Cam."

"Let's go to the party room,"

Aunt Molly said.

"Let's see some magic."

Chapter 2
Time for Magic

"It's time for Teddy,"

a woman called out.

"It's time for magic!"

"Hurry," Aunt Molly

told Cam and Eric.

"There are seats in the back."

A short, fat man wearing a big top hat

and long cape came into the room.

"That's Teddy," Aunt Molly whispered.

Teddy shook his hands,

and feathers fell to the floor.

People cheered.

Teddy took a bottle off a table.

He poured milk

from the bottle into a cup.

He held the cup upside down,

and no milk spilled out.

People cheered again.

Teddy bowed.

He put his hat on the table.

Then he reached in

and took out a live bird.

"This is Oscar," Teddy said.

Oscar flapped his wings

and everyone cheered.

Teddy put Oscar in the hat.

Teddy waved his hands over the hat.

Then he held it up
and Oscar was gone.
The hat was empty.

Teddy put the hat on his head.
He bowed, and everyone cheered.
"Have fun shopping," Teddy said.
People left until only Teddy, Molly,
Cam, and Eric were in the room.

"Hey, Molly," Teddy said.

"I'm glad you came."

"That was a great show," Eric said.

"Thank you."

Teddy opened a secret flap
in the middle of the table
and reached in.

"Hey," Teddy said.

"Where's Oscar?"

Chapter 3
Oscar Is a Clever Bird

"You made him disappear,"

Aunt Molly said.

"No, I didn't," Teddy said.

He showed Molly a secret flap

in his hat.

"I pushed him through here

and into a box hidden in the table.

Right after each show I put him back

in this cage with all his toys."

Eric reached into the box.

"Hey, I found a feather."

Cam reached in.

"This box has lots of doors," she said.

"And one is open."

Teddy saw the small open door

at the side of the table.

The walls around the party room
didn't go all the way to the ceiling.
"This is terrible," Teddy said.
"Oscar could be anywhere
in the store.
He could even have flown out
and be lost in the mall."
"Don't worry," Aunt Molly
told her friend.

"But who will feed him?"

Teddy asked.

"Who will talk to him?

Who will tell him he's a clever bird?"

"Don't worry," Molly said again.

"Cam is clever, too.

She'll find Oscar."

"Hey," Eric said. "What about me?"

Molly said, "Yes, Eric.

You're a clever boy.

We'll all find Oscar."

Chapter 4
Cam Said, "Click!"

There were lots of large pipes
near the ceiling.

"Where do those pipes go?"
Eric asked.

"Everywhere," Teddy said,
and waved his arms.

"They go all over the store."

"Oscar could be resting
on top of a pipe," Cam said.

"But we can't see up there."

"Wait," Teddy said.

"Wait right here."

Teddy hurried out of the room.

He came back with a small

stepladder and a broom.

He stepped up and banged on the

pipes with the broom.

Clang! Clang!

"Oscar! It's your friend, Teddy!"

Clang! Clang!

Everyone looked up.

They waited.

But they didn't see Oscar.

Molly said, "Maybe he's looking

at the video games.

Everyone likes video games."

Teddy said, "Maybe

he's with the puppets."

They looked in the

video game part of the store.

They didn't find Oscar.

Then they looked

in the puppet area.

Aunt Molly put a lion puppet on one

hand and a rabbit on the other.

"What's the best thing to put

in a pie?" the lion puppet asked.

"Your teeth,"

the rabbit puppet answered.

"What's yellow and jumpy?"

the rabbit asked.

"A banana with hiccups,"

the lion answered.

"Pies, bananas," Cam said.

"Those are snacks.

I have an idea."

Cam closed her eyes

and said, "Click!"

Molly told Teddy about the pictures

in Cam's head.

"Wow!" Teddy said.

"That's like magic."

Cam opened her eyes.

"I think I know where to find Oscar,"

she said.

"I may have solved this mystery."

Chapter 5
A Game of Memory

"Aunt Molly's riddles

made me think of food," Cam said.

"Then you clocked and saw Oscar.

Where is he?" Teddy asked.

"Is he scared?

Does he miss me?"

"Cam didn't clock!" Eric told Teddy.

"She clicked!"

"And I didn't see Oscar," Cam said.

"I looked at a picture of the sign with the arrows.

One points to snacks."

"Are you hungry?" Molly asked.

"No, but birds are always hungry," Cam said.

"Teddy's Toys has popcorn.

I can even smell it.

Birds like popcorn.

Oscar might be in the snack area."

They all went to the snack area.

"There he is," Teddy said.

"There's Oscar!"

He was eating bits of popcorn that had fallen on the floor.

Teddy held out his hand and called,

"Come to Teddy!"

Oscar flew to him.

"I was worried about you,"

Teddy said.

He put Oscar in his cage.

Then he told Oscar about Cam's

great memory.

"Come with me," Teddy said

to Cam, Eric, and Molly.

"I have a reward to give you
for finding my clever bird."
They followed Teddy to another part
of the store.
Teddy gave them each a game.
"Thank you," Cam, Eric, and Molly
said to Teddy.
"Mine is a memory game," Eric said.
"I love memory games.

But I won't play this with Cam.

She'd always win."

"Clock!" Teddy said.

"No, click!" Cam said, and laughed.

"Click! Click!" Cam, Eric, Molly, and Teddy said.

"Click! Click!"

A Cam Jansen Memory Game

Take another look at the picture on page 6.
Study it.
Blink your eyes and say, "Click!"
Then turn back to this page
and answer these questions:

1. What color is Cam's jacket?

2. Who is walking in front,
   Cam or Eric?

3. There's a bookstore in the picture.
   What's its name?

4. Is anyone in the picture waving his
   or her hand?

5. What color is Aunt Molly's jacket?